For Laurence
−CL
*For Diane, Grahame
and Amy*
−GH

tiger tales
An imprint of ME Media LLC
202 Old Ridgefield Road
Wilton, CT 06897
First published in the United States 2001
Originally published in Great Britain 2000
as *The Gift of Christmas*
by Little Tiger Press, London
Text © 2000 Christine Leeson
Illustration © 2000 Gaby Hansen
ISBN 1-58925-011-7
CIP data available
First US Edition
Printed in Dubai
1 3 5 7 9 10 8 6 4 2

THE MAGIC OF CHRISTMAS

by Christine Leeson

Illustrated by Gaby Hansen

tiger tales

It was Molly Mouse's first Christmas. The sky was streaked with pink and gold, and there was a tingle in the air.

Through the window of a house something was shining and glittering into the night.

"What is that, Mom?" asked Molly.

"It's a Christmas tree," said her mother. "People cover it with shiny balls, lights, and stars."

"I wish *we* had a Christmas tree," sighed Molly.

"Why don't you go into the woods to find one?" said her mother. "You could make it look just as nice as that tree in the window."

Molly thought this was a great idea. She called her brothers and sisters together, and off they all scampered.

On the way to the woods, they came to a barn. The mice rummaged through it, looking for something to add to their tree. Under a big pile of hay, Molly found a doll.

"This is like the doll on the top of the Christmas tree in the window," she said. "It will be just right for our tree."

But the doll belonged to someone else.

"Grr!" said the old farm dog. "That's mine!"

"Don't chase us!" cried Molly. "I only thought the doll would look nice on our Christmas tree."

The old dog yawned. It was true that sometimes he chased mice. But because it was Christmas, or because he remembered the Christmas tree in the farmhouse and how he used to play with the children there, he said the mice could borrow the doll.

The mice left the barn and walked across the barnyard, carrying the doll. They came to the edge of the woods.

"Hey," Molly shouted. "I see something else we can put on our Christmas tree!" It was a gold ribbon, hanging from a branch of an oak tree. Molly scampered up the trunk, took hold of the ribbon, and pulled.

But the ribbon belonged to a magpie.
She had taken it to line her nest.
"Please don't be angry," said Molly.
"I only wanted the gold ribbon for our
Christmas tree."

Usually the magpie chased mice. But because it
was Christmas, or because she had also been
admiring the Christmas tree in the window, she let
go of the other end of the ribbon. Molly took the
ribbon thankfully.

In the distance Molly saw some shiny round things lying on the ground. They were like the shiny balls on the Christmas tree in the window.

"Exactly what we want!" cried Molly, running to pick one of them up. "Now we have a doll, a gold ribbon, and a shiny ball!"

But those shiny balls belonged to a fox. "Those are my crab apples," he barked. "I'm saving them for the cold days ahead."

"We only thought one would look good on our Christmas tree," said Molly, trembling.

The fox sniffed. He chased mice most of the time. But because it was Christmas, or because he had never seen a Christmas tree before, he went back into the woods. Molly picked up a shiny crab apple and carried it away.

Twilight was falling as the mice went deeper into the woods. There, in the middle of a bramble bush, they could see a shining star and a dozen tiny lights glittering green and gold.

"Stars for our tree!" shouted Molly. "Let me get them." But when Molly reached into the bush, she found not stars...

but a collar, belonging to an angry mother cat. She had her kittens with her and their three pairs of eyes shone in the dark.

"Oh no!" gulped Molly. "I only wanted something sparkly for our Christmas tree."

The cat pricked her ears. She always chased mice. But because it was Christmas, or because she remembered the Christmas tree in the cozy home where she'd been a kitten, the mother cat slipped off her collar. She let the mice have it for their tree.

At last, in a clearing in the
deepest part of the woods,
the mice found a large evergreen
tree. "Our Christmas tree!"
cried Molly. They hung the doll,
the ribbon, the crab apple,
and the cat's collar on the
tree's branches.

"Oh," said Molly
when they had finished.
"It doesn't look at all
like the tree I saw in
the window." Sadly
the mice turned away.
Disappointed, they
walked all the
way back home
and went straight
to bed.

In the middle of the night the mother mouse woke up Molly and her brothers and sisters. "Come with me," she whispered. "I have something to show you."

The mice scurried along behind their mother, past the farm and into the woods. Other animals hurried on ahead of them, into the deepest part of the woods.

At last the mice reached the clearing
where Molly's Christmas tree was. Molly
stood completely still. Her eyes grew
large and round.

"Oh, look at that!" she cried.

During the night the animals had all added decorations to the Christmas tree. The frost had come and touched everything with glitter. The little tree sparkled, and even the stars in the sky seemed to be caught in its branches, with the biggest and brightest star right at the very top.

"Our Christmas tree is even better than the one in window," whispered Molly happily.

And because it was Christmas, all the animals from the woods sat quietly around the tree, at peace with each other.